rdec re

This book belongs ies

....

Note to parents and carers

Read it yourself is a series of classic, traditional tales, written in a simple way to give children a confident and successful start to reading.

Each book is carefully structured to include many high-frequency words that are vital for first reading. The sentences on each page are supported closely by pictures to help with reading, and to offer lively details to talk about.

The books are graded into four levels that progressively introduce wider vocabulary and longer stories as a reader's ability grows.

Ideas for use

- Begin by looking through the book and talking about the pictures. Has your child heard this story before?

- Help her with any words she does not know, either by helping her to sound them out or supplying them yourself.

- Developing readers can be concentrating so hard on the words that they sometimes don't fully grasp the meaning of what they're reading. Answering the puzzle questions on pages 30 and 31 will help with understanding.

For more information and advice, visit www.ladybird.com/readityourself

Level 2 is ideal for children who have received some reading instruction and can read short, simple sentences with help.

Special features:

Careful match between story and pictures

Short, simple sentences

Large, clear type

One day, a nut fell on Chicken Licken.

"Ouch! The sky is falling down!" said Chicken Licken. "I must tell the king."

On the way, they met Ducky Lucky.

"The sky is falling down," said Chicken Licken. "I'm going to tell the king."

Frequent repetition of main story words and phrases

Educational Consultant: Geraldine Taylor

A catalogue record for this book is available from the British Library

Published by Ladybird Books Ltd
80 Strand, London, WC2R 0RL
A Penguin Company

002 - 10 9 8 7 6 5 4 3 2
© LADYBIRD BOOKS LTD MMXI
Ladybird, Read It Yourself and the Ladybird Logo are registered or
unregistered trade marks of Ladybird Books Limited.

ISBN: 978-1-40930-716-7

Printed in China

Chicken Licken

Illustrated by Richard Johnson

One day, a nut fell on Chicken Licken.

"Ouch! The sky is falling down!" said Chicken Licken. "I must tell the king."

On the way, he met
Henny Penny.

"The sky is falling down,"
said Chicken Licken.
"I'm going to tell the king."

"I'll come too,"
said Henny Penny.

And off they went to
find the king.

To the Castle

11

On the way, they met
Cocky Locky.

"The sky is falling down,"
said Chicken Licken.
"I'm going to tell the king."

"I'll come too,"
said Cocky Locky.

And off they went to
find the king.

14

To the Castle

On the way, they met Ducky Lucky.

"The sky is falling down," said Chicken Licken. "I'm going to tell the king."

16

"I'll come too,"
said Ducky Lucky.

And off they went to
find the king.

18

19

On the way, they met
Drakey Lakey.

"The sky is falling down,"
said Chicken Licken.
"I'm going to tell the king."

"I'll come too,"
said Drakey Lakey.

And off they went to
find the king.

Farm

To the Castle

23

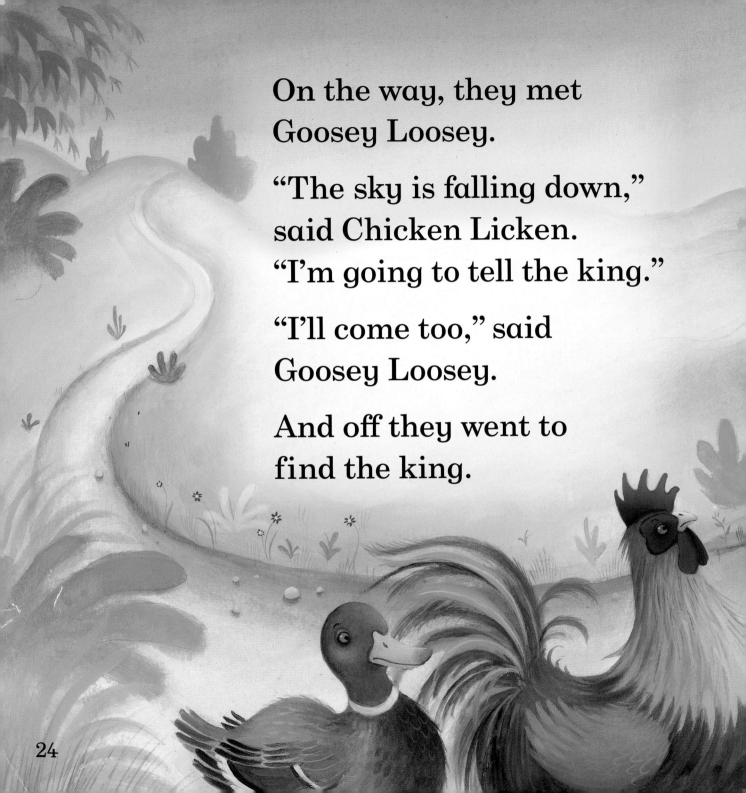

On the way, they met Goosey Loosey.

"The sky is falling down," said Chicken Licken. "I'm going to tell the king."

"I'll come too," said Goosey Loosey.

And off they went to find the king.

25

On the way, they met
Foxy Loxy.

"The sky is falling down,"
they said. "We're going to
tell the king."

"The king lives here,"
said Foxy Loxy.
"Follow me."

To the Castle

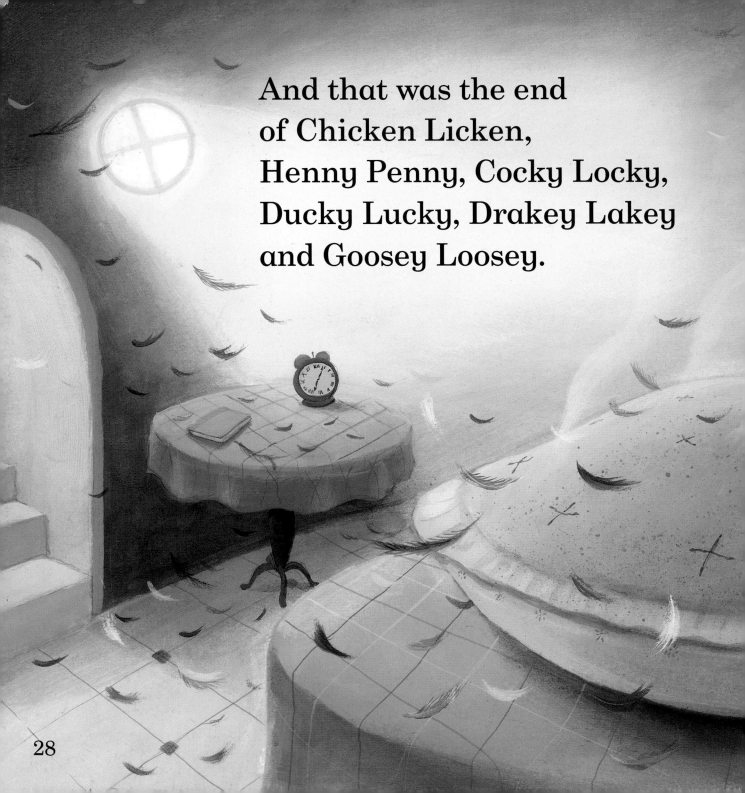

And that was the end
of Chicken Licken,
Henny Penny, Cocky Locky,
Ducky Lucky, Drakey Lakey
and Goosey Loosey.

How much do you remember about the story of Chicken Licken? Answer these questions and find out!

- What falls on Chicken Licken's head?

- What does he think is happening?

- Who does Chicken Licken go to tell?

- Where does Foxy Loxy take everyone?

Look at the pictures, then match them to the story words.

Chicken Licken

Henny Penny

Ducky Lucky

Goosey Loosey

Foxy Loxy

Read it yourself
with Ladybird

The Three Billy Goats Gruff

Cinderella

Little Red Hen

Goldilocks and the Three Bears

The Enormous Turnip

The Magic Porridge Pot

The Ugly Duckling

The Gingerbread Man

Sleeping Beauty

Little Red Riding Hood

Sly Fox and Red Hen

The Three Little Pigs

Town Mouse and Country Mouse

Chicken Licken

The Elves and the Shoemaker

Jack and the Beanstalk

Hansel and Gretel

The Pied Piper of Hamelin

The Wizard of Oz

Heidi

Collect all the titles in the series.